ROSELAND FARM ADVENTURES:
HALLOWED BEGINNINGS

JENNIFER SNELL

Published by Mindstir Media, LLC
45 Lafayette Rd | Suite 181| North Hampton, NH 03862 | USA
1.800.767.0531 | www.mindstirmedia.com

Printed in the United States of America
ISBN-13: 978-1-7363845-5-8

In Dedication To:

All the health care professionals we met along our way who went above and beyond in offering their time, talent, knowledge, love, care, and hope for Eliza's beginning in the world.

The Ronald McDonald House Charities who provided care and comfort to us during our troubling time.

My husband for not just being my best friend and soulmate, but the person whom I have come to rely on in my most desperate times and who continues to support, love, guide, and provide wisdom for me.

And lastly, my most beautiful creation and person, and with whom I share the love that can only be understood by the Creator Himself and me, Eliza Wren.

To donate to the RMHC organization, please visit:
https://rmhc.org/expansion

Book's Purpose and Mission:

Hallowed Beginnings was written to act as a resource, especially for those experiencing time spent in the NICU, with their own struggles and story regarding the birth of their child. I hope that my words can spark, not only the imagination for adults and children alike, but remind us all of the important life lessons, the individual struggles we deal with, and the unique and powerful abilities we each possess to make a positive change for ourselves and others with what we encounter along our life's journey. Lastly, may this book and these resources offer proof for the miracles, intentions, and love behind God's plan for us all so that we confidently ask for that help as we need it along our way.

Foreword:

One thing we can all agree on is that, throughout our lives, we are presented with challenges that can create a very dark and vulnerable place for us, where we are forced to make a decision or act as a witness where control is out of our hands.

After eight years of praying for a child to bless our lives, the time had come in which God saw we were ready. Eliza chose us from among many quality candidates that she and God discussed for her well-being, protection, and development in life. She was delicately implanted in my womb, which acted as a protective eggshell, for what I thought would be a normal nine months of pregnancy, bliss, and pain I had ever so patiently waited for. Little did I know that Eliza's plan was to begin her mission and make her appearance early in life . . . Three months early, to be exact! At twenty-seven weeks, Eliza Wren made her way into the world. On that day, she blessed the lives of many and would impact the lives of many more along her way—more than just her mother and father. We had been carefully selected to support her and guide her, and we watched in amazement as she surprised us with the gifts she was given and meant to share.

Our journey as parents began much differently than the way we had so anticipated and for which we had set our expectations, realistic or not. Like any parents who have their set of hopes and dreams for their child, you also house a set of dark worries that sometimes takes precedence over your reactions and ability to take healthy action. Casey and I had to quickly rationalize and reimagine the world for which we had dreamed and prayed for our daughter. Now, we were forced to quickly learn, understand, and use in our daily language, medical lingo and jargon as we joined the fight for our daughter's survival. We were challenged along the way to research, explore, and question the care for our daughter in hopes for the best possible outcome.

We all react a certain way in a time of crisis. Upon the approach of my daughter's first birthday, I am now able to fully reflect on and understand, not only how I respond in the moment of crisis in my life, but the resources I choose to invest in and access first to assist me along the way. Even though we didn't realize its importance or necessity in our lives at that time, Casey and I also soon learned that the support we were searching for, and in such desperate need of, was a very slim and selective market to choose from.

So, my intention as the author of this book is to provide a gift of comfort and to help you remember the magic that exists, and is intentionally made for us to have. It blesses our lives in the times we need it most. For me, the journey as a parent began with being a caretaker to a micro-preemie—a category in itself meant to represent a human being even smaller and more unimaginable than that of the original classification and miracle of a preemie.

I wish to share my testimony to provide the lessons that I learned along the way to help those in a similar situation as mine. I also want to act as a visible and living reminder and resource for anyone searching for that long-lost, dormant, yet ever-so-comforting feeling of the magic behind having hope, and the capabilities and powers we are each uniquely gifted with. These gifts were bestowed well before our creation, and are meant to make a positive and impactful change within ourselves and perhaps in others. This allows us to grow into the reflection of love and light God so meant for us to believe in and live as.

The story of the lost kittens and their adventures on the farm with their human family is based on true events and told directly from an eyewitness account.

Once Upon a Time . . .

On a typical summer's day on a small, rural farm named Roseland located alongside the rolling hills of Kansas, the day was coming to a close, and the night's chorus of creatures began their song. Tucked inside safe and sound the farmhouse is the Snell family—Farmer Casey, Mother Jenni, and their daughter, Eliza Wren. At the foot of their ever-so-small bed, their two chocolate lab canines, Taz and Margot, occupy the remaining space in the bed and provide extra warmth the family did not need on this hot and humid summer's night. But, as you will learn, the Snell family made many sacrifices out of love for their dear pets on their farm. As the night carries them into a deep lull and swiftly away to dreamland, the hours pass to a new day's beginning and its purpose.

Outside, tucked cozily within their own house for a restful night's slumber as well, is Mother Cat and her four kittens, snoozing away side by side in the fresh strewn straw. The kittens were wistfully dreaming of the next day's activities of batting moths and butterflies, stalking moles, mice, and frogs, and enjoying their morning and afternoon milk with their mother.

Eliza had raised these kittens from birth and the kittens and Eliza shared a very special connection upon their entry into the world. Eliza was born at twenty-seven weeks. That's three months early from her original expected arrival time! She was only twelve inches long and weighed a mere one pound and twelve ounces. Throughout her three-and-a-half-month stay in the NICU, Eliza demonstrated just how resilient she was and her willingness to fight for her life's purpose. Eventually, Eliza was welcomed home to Roseland where the real adventure awaited her.

The kittens were quite the surprise themselves. For, like the wonder and excitement in a child's eyes on Christmas morning, the kittens were a special gift for Miss Eliza Wren and for the rest of the Snell family as they would soon come to learn.

Seasons passed and each new one began with Eliza assisting Mother Cat daily with the care of the kittens. Casey, Jenni and Eliza enjoyed watching the kittens develop their own individual personalities and provide their unique contributions to the farm.

First, there was Wednesday—a female calico with many orange and black stripes throughout her soft and buttery coat. She was born with a very brave heart and a deep curiosity.

Second was Perdita—another female calico but with black and white stripes throughout her equally soft and buttery coat. Perdita was much smaller than her siblings and fought from birth to keep up during feedings and playing. She never showed exhaustion or frustration, or let her size come between her and her goals.

Third was Tiger Lily—another female similar in color and markings to her sister, Wednesday. Tiger Lily, also much smaller than her siblings, had not only the same appetite as the two larger kittens, evidenced by her ever-so-plump little belly, but had the tenacity and strength to always accomplish her own goals.

And lastly, the fourth, Toulouse, the only male, was mostly white with orange and black on his ears and tail, and perfectly round splash of orange in the center of his back. A calico cat. Toulouse is very rare to come across being a male calico cat. Toulouse was born with great bravery and curiosity like that of his sister, Wednesday. However, Toulouse was also much more of a risk-taker in his choices and liked to push the limit when given the opportunity.

Little did these kittens know that this night would bring much trouble and change to the farm the very next morning.

In the wee hours of the morning, Farmer Casey and his family were abruptly awakened by bold and intrusive alerts from their trusting canines. Now, the family did jump out of bed together to investigate but treated the occasion like any other one they had experienced so many nights before. They assumed it was either an ornery opossum or a rascally raccoon causing havoc and taunting the dogs once again. If Mother had trusted her intuition on this matter, however, and had taken action or intervened, the next day's events might not have unfolded as they did.

As the sun slowly crept up over the horizon and greeted the little farm the next morning, Farmer Casey and his family went about the start of their day as usual, going about their chores and duties.

First, they greeted the cats and gave them their morning milk in a special little saucer as they preferred along with their breakfast of soft salmon and flaky tuna fish. Much to Mother's surprise, the breakfast table was missing a few members that fine morning. Toulouse and Wednesday had skipped breakfast, a very unusual act for these two on-the-go kittens who need their energy to fuel them through the day's events.

Mother and Eliza set off to search for the two lost kittens, calling out their names over and over in anticipation they'd see them running frantically back home to partake in their morning meal with their family! As time went on, and the hours grew longer, still no sign of Toulouse or Wednesday was to be had. Concern and worry loomed over the family like the storm clouds rolling in across the Kansas skies with which they were all too familiar. Mother and Eliza began to accept the fact that Toulouse and Wednesday might not come home tonight, or perhaps, the prior evening's events led to their untimely demise.

As the worst possible outcome began to sink in for the sad and concerned pair, the dimming likelihood for the safe return of the kittens shaped their reality. Days turned into nights, and life on the farm went about its usual way, though Mother and Eliza continued to look for the lost kittens every day, calling out their names in desperation, hoping to see them gleefully running towards their mother and home.

Meanwhile, Farmer Casey noticed how sad his family had become, for the absence of the lost kittens and their unique way of contributing to life on the farm left the family with much sorrow in their hearts. Farmer Casey reminded his loving wife and sorrowful daughter about an important lesson which helped them during a time when they most needed its power, assistance, and magic.

Farmer Casey reminded his family of a simple thing that brought magic to their lives when they least expected but greatly needed it—a gift from God called HOPE. Farmer Casey also reminded his family that hope is always there when we need it, but we are the only ones who can ask for its gift to be given and use it for its said intention. Farmer Casey lastly reminded his family that to do this, one must pray very hard to God and his warriors who have the power to answer prayers. He said, "We must believe in their work as visible miracles that act as a gift to bless our lives and assist us in becoming a reflection of God's love and light."

Mother and Eliza took what Farmer Casey said to heart that night as they went to bed and thought how silly they must have seemed not to have thought to pray in the beginning! Mother and Eliza prayed very hard that night to God and Mother Mary, and the many helpful saints and loved ones in heaven for the safe and quick return home of their lost kittens. For, during a time in Mother and Father's life, they too, had to rely on the magic of hope and the power of prayer to guide them through great uncertainty and fear upon the birth of the daughter, Eliza Wren, and her mission to accomplish and overcome as a micro-preemie. The same faith and belief Mother had then was put forth that night in prayer as she carefully and thoughtfully constructed words to be lifted up to the heavens and left in the hands of the almighty Creator and his warriors.

The next morning, the family was once again abruptly awakened by their canines alerting them to outside visitors. Mother crawled out of bed to soothe the dogs, investigate, and greet the unexpected visitors. To Mother's surprise, it was Aunt Joni and Uncle Carl! Uncle Carl was walking towards the cats' cozy shed and much confusion about the situation grew within Mother. She chose to further investigate by going outside and greeting them with a friendly, "Good morning!" and "How do you do?"

Mother noticed Uncle Carl holding something white and fluffy in one hand and in his other, he held a striped, orange calico kitten. Emotions flooded Mother's body, and that magical feeling of hope overtook her. Uncle Carl was holding none other than the brave, the curious, the almighty Toulouse and Wednesday! Uncle Carl announced that he had found Toulouse and his sister in the ditch as he was peering outside his window and admired them trying to befriend a very scared armadillo.

Mother couldn't help but shout for joy and give her praise to God for the miracle, and then she thanked Aunt Joni and Uncle Carl for their kind action and went back inside to announce the great news to the now-awake family.

Mother joyfully entered the room to share the miracle she had just witnessed and to thank her husband for reminding her of the magic that lies within each of us that, when accessed, provides us with visible proof of God's great love for us and all his living creatures.

Outside, Toulouse and Wednesday greeted their mother and received the same loving welcome from her with licking and purring and the intertwining of tails. They spent their afternoon re-adjusting and telling their tales of adventure and survival. They were reminded of a saying that hung framed within their cozy shed that said:

"When trials are greatest and all goes wrong,
Just buckle your armour and trudge along,
The way that is weary, dark and cold,
May lead to shelter, within the fold,
These trials were meant to make you strong:
So buckle your armour and trudge along."

And so, as resilient as Eliza Wren had become in her own beginning, Toulouse and Wednesday now share a similar story with a similar outcome, and it's all because they each believed in a little bit of magic. And to think that this all takes place before our creation as our own exclusive plan! And so as the days continue for the little family and their farm, daily thanks is given for the many blessings bestowed upon them including one they were left with—a very valuable lesson. This lesson is one that they have taken much to heart and choose to act upon daily, sharing it as a testimony to others, leaving them with the peace, joy, and comfort they seek as a happy little family.

Author Biography:

Jennifer Snell is a freelance writer of non-fiction, including stories meant to impact children and families through personal life experiences. She is completing her doctoral studies in the area of Adult and Lifelong Learning through the University of Arkansas. Her goal upon the completion of her doctoral degree, she will continue to write children's stories and plans to stay in the education field.

She lives on her historical farm, Roseland, in Kansas with her husband, daughter, two chocolate labs, farm cats, and many other livestock animals. Apart from writing, her hobbies include: Gardening, traveling, photography, and advocating support for those experiencing time in the NICU.

Please visit www.frontierwife.org to access her blog, whose articles are intended to produce positive change, reflection, and growth within us all.

CPSIA information can be obtained
at www.ICGtesting.com
Printed in the USA
LVHW072019290321
682893LV00002B/37